Thicker than Water

MELANIE MCCURDIE

Copyright © 2017 Melanie McCurdie

All rights reserved.

ISBN:0995887802
ISBN-13: 978-0-9958878-0-0

DEDICATION

The Locusts
BabyGirl
Voodoo Doll

For always

ACKNOWLEDGMENTS

My life is filled with the most fascinating, diverse and amazing bunch of individuals I could ever dream of calling friends and loved ones. You all mean so much to me.

For my friend and companion in literary crime, Foggy McCorrigan. Thanks for always lending your unique point of perception.

For Jim. You are a treasure beyond measure and a someone I am so glad to count amongst my friends Thanks for your suggestions and the like

And last, but never least, Amanda Marie. You are an incredible lady and one of my most favorite sisters. That smile and the Go Slay attitude keeps encouraging me to fight for my own dreams. Love you sweetie. To the moon xoxo

1

The sign on the door swings back and forth in the air-conditioned lobby; the arc of its enthusiastic movement slows, even as I thumb the lock and stand a moment in the light of the blazing summer sun, watching the small crowd that was gathering in the parking lot. Word travels fast in a small town and this time was no exception. I wonder idly why that is when no one here has had use of any device to do as much as text with.

I slide the flat of my palm along my right hip, smoothing the self-conscious wrinkles that my hand was sure were there. A thirty-pound weight loss in recent months has left my confidence sobbing on the floor, where I would rather be myself.

What a bunch of trained monkeys, I reflect, observing the awkward wiggle-walk of an o-so-mature teenage girl with rather large breasts and a vacant, come-hither stare.

The three suited men standing across from her ogle her nubile young curves and their piggish behaviour catches my eye. She leans against the front panel of my sweet Cherry Red Cuda and the sight of the keys hanging from her belt loops scraping against the paint makes me want to rip the little bitch's throat out. Soon enough, and if I was lucky, I would obliterate the little snatch and teach her a lesson about respect.

Someone behind me thumps in the quiet and the noise startles me back from my murderous plotting. A small silent crowd rustles like blackbirds on a branch, waiting, for my next move. The air feels thin as my hand becomes sweat and slick and the gun I had stolen begins to slip. Anxiously, I transfer it and wipe my left palm lightly down the length of my thigh. It's heavy and smells heavily of oil and testosterone. Of course it would, considering who I had taken it from. He wouldn't need it where he was going, and I was in need of a working weapon right now. I really had hoped that I had killed the motherfucker but a quick glance tells me that he should be regaining consciousness soon.

The moaning whine of the old woman is making me antsy and the sound of her labored breathing seems to be purposefully irritating. I turn on my heel with a grace that shocks me to stare down the elderly woman, secretly relishing the way she recoils with a wide-eyed terror that probably should upset me. It doesn't though. I haven't directly threatened anyone, yet; the gun in my hand I'd only vaguely waved in a menacing direction and they dropped to the floor like stones. Actions do indeed speak louder. These assholes have never listened to a word that I have uttered even once in their poor excuses for lives, and I've known them for all of mine. Such is the way of the privileged. They don't know what it means to suffer for anything.

That childlike anxiety in her eyes makes me feel a little bit bad for her, for them; after all, I was apparently in polite, civilized society and its hardly social convention to wave a loaded weapon at a bank full of the community's finest. That niggling humanity is nothing more than a fleeting fancy and is gone in a blink. Not one of the individuals in this room has ever given a tin shit about me when they were destroying my world. Why should I care if I destroy theirs?

I'm not a terrible person, or at least, I wasn't once upon a time` but right now I can't care anymore, not until I have the confirmation that I've nearly killed myself to get.

The sun is brutal even for July, and it burns the back of my neck through the untreated windows as I take in the faces of my unfortunate captives. Each is one I know as well as my own and behind each frightened expression lies a slyer, knowing smirk. They know exactly why they are here and think that they are smarter than I am. Look at them sitting there with their noses in the air and the lazy savoir faire imperviousness of the nouveau riche, the way they smirk amongst themselves Suddenly, as if from above, I inspired by the terrified masks they wear.

"What are you going to do to us!?" the querulous voice of the old woman rings out and echoes between the silences and shouts of the Hewe Police Force. A glance over my shoulder reveals a ton about how the boys in blue are managing. Several bumble about in the crowded parking; while several of them stand watching me watching them with their hands on the butts of their pistols.

Surely, were I a man, I would be dead by now but put the criminal in a dress that shows a little leg and some cleavage, and voila! They turn into teenage horn dogs without a brain to share. To my left more proof of their witlessness; two of the town's finest in blue bang off each other and fall on their asses in such an improvisational slapstick kind of way that I can't help but giggle out loud.

"Are you seriously laughing? Waving a loaded gun in the faces of the town council is amusing to you?!" God, I hate that woman. Tiffani Dexter. The pretty young matron around town, formerly Tiffani Howard is the Mayor's daughter, and was once the biggest whore at Richter High. According to the little blue book that I found in the bathroom one afternoon, she'd been down on every member of both football teams, the AV club and at least half of the teachers including the ultra-conservative Miss Clark. If I was to believe the book I still had and the notes there, combined with the fearful expression on Tiffani's face, I'll bet she walked weird for at least a week. Frigid my ass. I'm saving Tiff for last, and the whole town will hear her scream for mercy before I'm through.

"Well? Answer her Junie!" the old crone demands again in that snooty nasal whine that I despise, "What are you going to do to us?" She thinks she is better than I, better than anyone she views as lesser, when her soul is hardly lily white. Allowing her to show off again and allowing her to get away with it would set a poor example. I consider killing her as sort of an object lesson to the rest and entertain the thought more aggressively as the hag grows more agitated. Her son Victor places his hand on her injured cheek and glares out the window at the sun that was finally beginning to descend a little in the sky.

The born-again virgin, realizing she has support, adds a strident whine to her complaints. Some things never change. I fire a shot at the old woman that goes purposefully wide, and smile as a chip of the custom marble tile closest to her right elbow flies up and slices her cheek open. The collar of the high-necked white blouse she wears turns a bright red in no time and it nearly glows in the natural light. With her thin lips forming a perfect O that accentuates her wrinkles, she lifts her hand to her cheek, where her fingers trace the lips of the wound that gapes like a small mouth.

"I haven't decided Mrs. Kartish, but perhaps, you could shut your piehole while I think about it.." Her mouth trembles; it closes then opens again like a landlocked fish and her hands shake as tears fall from her rheumy eyes. "Stop looking so shocked, this is partly your fault. I tried so hard not to hate you. Any of you. There was so much time and effort wasted, just to play nice; you made me a pawn in a game only you could win and you didn't have the decency to tell me. Not having to pretend anymore feels so much better than acting like a fool for you," I say to no one in particular and to each them. I didn't shout, but spoke in a thoughtful conversational tone without raising my voice an octave.

The tip of the gun is still warm, and the old woman attempts to pull away from me with a frightened whine. My hand on the back of her neck keeps that from happening and the barrel pressed hard into the fleshy waddle under her chin is enough to make my point.

"Keep. Your. Mouth. Shut. Or the next time you open it will be your last. Give me a thumb up if you understand."

She gives an enthusiastic response and I smack her with the butt of the gun in the left temple for her effort. Her husband is cursing and waving his feeble arms around like an angry bumblebee. At least *she* will be quiet for a while. If he keeps it up, he will be next to her. I need to consider a few other things before the fun starts.

They clamor around her as I consider my choices. They few, but at least I have some. As I see the situation, there are only a few avenues open to me at this stage. I could take my pound of flesh, kill myself and let them believe they survived me. I could kill them all, which is my preference. Or I could force the cops to do it.

No matter what I decide, I am a walking corpse who has yet begun to rot and nothing else matters but that confirmation of death. Sick of the scene in front of me, I turn away, brushing my hair from my eyes and scanning the crowd for the cunt that scratched my car. I still owe her a lesson.

2

Twin holes burn in my head; heavy disapproval weights the stare. I can deal with that, after all, taking shots at old women is hardly acceptable behaviour and something that society frowns upon.

What is uncomfortable, however, is the awareness eyes like fingers stripping away my clothing and the excruciating sensation my flesh being peeled away, first lustfully then with vicious intent. "Stop eyeballing me Timmy. I hate it." That knowing chuckle that has always made me crazy rolls through the place, lightly mocking as I curse inside and cock the gun. I'll blow his fucking head off for being a dickhead. I was sure the bastard was still unconscious. I need to pay attention.

"What are you going to do about it? Take another shitty shot at Mom? Kill me? Fuck me? You know you want to. You never could resist the way I..."

Tiffani interrupts, gasping and I fight the urge to blow her damned stupid head off. *She needs to be last.* I remind myself again.

Oh, but that smug son of a bitch. I want to cut his throat now just to end the self-confident show but then, he is more useful to me in another capacity. It didn't mean he couldn't learn a lesson, however. "Shut it. And you're right. I never could resist and neither could you. She was never going to be enough for you, and you know it. But hey sweetling, you aren't in charge here. I am. The next outburst and she gets a prize."

Watching Tiffani's round brown eyes bulge unattractively in their sockets as I wave my weapon in her direction is such a delight. He chuckles again and I can feel his eyes like a tongue on my thighs and between. It pisses me off and I let out a frustrated groan. "I warned you. Dammit Timmy, you never listen to me." For fuck sake –

The right side of Tiffani's head explodes in a spray of shredded brain tissue, blood and bone, covering the horrified screaming faces of those closest.

Her body jitters uncontrollably with her heels slapping in rapid tempo on the floor then it relaxes along with her sphincter and bladder. Her blood is much darker than I expected it to be. Thicker too. What little mind she possessed is now a mess on the floor. "Any more questions?"

The only sound is muffled vomiting and the silence is a relief after the ambient hum of the air conditioning and the human sounds of my hostages. The shrill ringing of the telephone shatters what little peace I'd gained. Naturally it would be the Chief of Police, that fucking moron. "Someone pick that up. Watch what you say." Timmy slowly gets to his feet and reaches over the counter with his eyes on mine and clears his throat before barking, "Yes?" into the receiver.

I can hear the frantic questions the Chief is asking and although I can't hear actual words, the tone conveys enough. "Mrs. T. Kartish. Yes. Yes, I'm sure! Her head is all over the damned floor. Is that sure enough?" Timmy's voice cracks slightly. I would swear on a stack of Stephen King novels that I hear humor though the down-turned corners of his full lips tell a different story.

"Mrs. Oliva Kartish has a cut cheek and is unconscious. No, she's not injured badly." He listens a moment and blinks out the window in disbelief, then around at the four remaining captives. "Absolutely not, Chief Sawton. Are you nuts?"

I grab the phone and point to the floor with the barrel of the gun and Timmy drops without giving me a second look. Good. The Chief is yelling in frustration about his plan and I slam it down hard enough to make the desk shiver. "Junie." I don't want to hear another word and observe two of the chief's boys in blue right outside the doors. "It's not enough for you that you stole everything from me, is it?" His head is shaking slowly back and forth and his spoiled Ivy League younger brother Victor starts laughing low and mean while gesturing at the cop to the left of the door with a knowing expression. "Say goodbye to your brother Timmy."

Victor stops laughing immediately and shrugs her shoulders, and with a roar, charges at me. I don't hesitate and pull the trigger. "Junie NO!"

The top of Victor's head flies apart much like his sister-in-law's had, but the bullet didn't hit low enough. My aim was off and now he is laughing and shuffling his feet as he spins around and around with the blood trickling over the edge of his shattered skull. He is dancing like a demented doll and singing while his father cries in his hands and his brother just watches sickly. This wasn't my intention.

"Jesus Junie," Timmy whispers sickly from the floor beside me, "just. Just end it okay? Junie, please." I can hear the tears in his voice and watch nauseated when Victor turns to me points with a shaky finger.

"Ohhhh JUUUUUUUUNIE," Victor sings in a garbled sing-song voice, his eyeballs bulging when his hands flutter like birds to sink into his brain; he screams as he begins pulling handfuls of the grey-pink tissue from the ruined shell of his mind. "YOU DID THIS TO ME! ASSBAG! CUMDUMPSTER! YOOOOOOOOOOOOOU DID IT!: Then, in confidential, sly aside, the ruined man false whispered, "Your little girl liked every second of wh-"

It is sufficient and I can't stand to listen to his filthy mouth any longer. A bullet to his right eye ends his shitty singing. The officers have dropped their weapons in shock and I take the opportunity to end them as well. Two shots, and two hats fly in the air and twin geysers of scarlet stain the sidewalk.

"You, Pops, get your scrawny old ass up off the floor, pick up that phone and call the Chief. If that," and here I stab him with my glare and gesture with the barrel of my own weapon towards the shattered windows, "happens again, I will cut off every one of your fingers and your tongue and shove it up your daughter-in-law's snatch. They were up there often enough it should feel like home. Make sure the Chief understands that all your deaths will be on his head. I will kill your wife and your son. I will cut you apart and then let you live. Do you understand me?"

The old man's hand slips in the blood trying to stand and he lands face first on the expensive marble that has caused more than one injury in this place. He lays there sobbing for a moment and then pushes himself up to his knees, using Tiffani's body as leverage.

The old fool squeaks when he realized and wipes his palm on his silk trousers before finally getting his ass off the floor. "Pops? I asked you if you understood."

He freezes and then nods without a word, familiarly typing the code that will allow him access to the phone and the cash drawers with no shake in his fingers whatsoever. "Pops." I hear my own voice loud in my ears and watch him shudder but never break stride. "I know what you've been doing. One fuck up and I will make sure that children scream when they see you on the street, and that women vomit." Timmy's hand finds my ankle and I look down into his miserable face. I want to feel something. I really do want to feel anything but I can't. I have nothing left to give.

"June. Please." Pretty words won't change a thing, not now. If he hadn't abandoned me, I might have never been in this position. I might have left off and let this all go. But that was then. His hand drops away and I lash out to kick him twice in the gut with the pointed toe of my shoe. "I have felt *that* every day for the past three months. Hurts, doesn't it?"

3

I had been only half listening to the patriarch when his holier-than-thou kicked in and then the old pervert had my full attention. "Just shoot her Orval. Two of your idiots are dead because you won't do what you committed to do. Pull the fucking trigger or you might as well blow your own head off. You'll wish you did." The front window is gone and the shards of broken glass fly through the lobby like bullets. Timmy has me on the ground, covering my body with his weight and taking the sharp spray to save my hide. "Get away from me," I rasp in his face, and shove him away, "your father wants me dead. He planned this as much as I did Timmy. Then slowly took everything from me. You. Let. Him… so get the fuck off me!" This time I pistol whip him and scramble away before he can trap me again. Motherfucker has a hard head.

"Hey Pops!"

The old bastard makes his first mistake and lets me know exactly where he is. The second mistake was losing his nerve and bolting from relative safety. I cut his ass down with a bullet to the leg and watch him skid and curl up on the floor. He moans and screams like a rich girl forced to clean toilets. "Coming Pops. Just hang tight daddy-o. I have one small thing -" I sing and crouch beside Timmy to smile into his starry-eyed expression. I may have hit him too hard. "I could have left when you did you know. But they," I gestured behind me with the pistol and genuinely smiled when the crone cries out, "convinced me to stay. Your daddy was the one who introduced me to Asher. He was also the one who killed him, in that office right back there. Blew his brains out all over the wall while our daughter watched in her stroller, but you know that, so don't look at me like I don't have reason."

Patriarch Pete is still whining. Jesus, he bitches hard. He isn't really hurt bad enough to die, although if he doesn't quit the howling I might blow his face off just to get a moment's peace. His wife has joined him and has her hand over his mouth in an attempt to stop his noise.

"Shut up Peter. She's coming," the hag says in a dead voice and I feel that righteous swelling in my chest. His blathering stops as his head falls to the side as I approach.

"June. Please you don't understand – "

"Save it Petey. *You* don't understand. -You may live in a small town but your ethics are big city. I know everything. Your employer, Frederick Elias, was very forthcoming with information Pete. It is truly amazing what a little incentive can bring. You are an extremely naughty boy. I suspect its time to have a chat with Olivia here." The shock that crosses her face would be hilarious if it weren't so pitiful, and she looks past me to where her son lays quietly, then into the face of her husband.

Outside the shattered windows, I can hear the chief yelling at his minions to keep it down and then continuing yelling his plans. This place is a fucking zoo and I have things to do before I walk out of here. "If you try to run, any of you, I will kill you no matter where you run to. Behave yourselves and I may just let you go." I have no intentions of letting any of them live but it is enough to give them hope, and I see it in their eyes.

Pops graciously left the gate open when he flew from safety and saved me from having to force the code from him. I am tired now and out of habit snag my purse from the counter where I had left it. The old fella had shown me a secret cache of cash years ago, and the other valuables that he claimed not even his wife was aware of. I have no doubt that Timmy does and that Victor did before his mind became spray.

Behind me the air conditioning thumps and a fresh breeze of cool air travels across my bare legs that makes me shiver. I blink and shake my head to clear it. This was no time to daydream. I had to get back to business. I still had three to kill here and then the added bonus of the coppers outside, all still immersed in a giant circle jerk just outside the building. The desk is an old relic from somewhere or another. Pops told me that too when he showed me his treasure trove and told me a few truths about what my life would entail should I marry his son. Ingenious design it truly was, some engineer's brainchild I suppose, and the poor thing ended up here in the Kartish whorehouse.

I can't help myself and crouch down to run my finger along the barely perceptible line that matches the grain of the wood. Just one more move and I can finish here, and live out the rest of my life in peace. Using the desk edge for leverage, I move quietly to my feet and around the side towards the last thing waiting in my path.

Timmy grabs me in the darkened office, pushing me forward until my face is against the wall and he breathes laughter into my ear before spinning me around. I knew daydreaming would cause trouble and here is proof. He had snuck in while I was reminiscing and now I can feel him hard against my belly, his hot and insistent erection letting me know exactly what was in store. There is no way in hell I was going to let him lay me. Not in here, not now and most certainly not again. . Once upon a time I would already be assuming his favorite position but now. No. But his hands feel good, the way they travel everywhere, warm on my ass and the way they pull my dress up to my hips.

"Nothing has changed," he growls into my ear after finding me bare. True to form and with no preamble, his fingers slide roughly into my body. No nothing has changed and he shamelessly brings me quickly to orgasm. "You never could resist." I never could resist. I could swear he was a demon; the way I was trapped from the first smile. I never could resist the way he took me over, and I am helpless at his mercy.

I can't resist; not the way his fingers pleasure me until my knees gave out, nor the way he tongues circles my clit like some slippery starving creature. With that combined sensation, no girl could stand a chance, least of all me. I nearly drown him in my pleasure and he chuckles again, that same smug, annoying laugh that still makes me want to bash his fucking head in. Or I would have had he not effectively, quite cleverly, disarmed me.

His beast has been released and the soft tip teases along my slit, searching for entry and I dart forward to whisper in his ear. I am quite clever too. Yes, admittedly, I want it as much has he very clearly does and woman is not meant to live without intercourse;

sexual or otherwise. I despise that I am still so weak. It doesn't matter when he carries my weight easily to his father's desk and slides his blade deep into my sheath as I am set down.

"Like the first time, Junie. Remember?" He huffs into my face with each thrust and I nod, riding the desire train while I plot his end. It feels like he was slamming his entire weight into my cunny and I just can't help myself. God help me, I buck back with all my strength, and lacerate his back with my nails when I cum. "Just like old times," I snarl back, digging deeper and enjoying the surprised displeasure that colors his eyes. He hated it then too and predictably he increases his tempo, ready to drop his seed once again and that is something that I have no intentions of letting happen.

"Where is my daughter, Timmy?" I whisper in his ear and laugh when he freezes in mid-thrust and his proud member trembles then wilts inside me. So, he does know. Admittedly, this whole scenario was pre-meditated, down to the sun soaked parking spot and this little interlude.

The fact was that it was he that could never resist, and I've spent three months plotting and searching for my little girl. I even bought a little house under an assumed name, in a quiet place in preparation for the day she comes home.

I did try to play ball, I did my best to play the game and still it wasn't enough. Now he is staring at me in horror and backs away with his spent member flopping gamely. I feel bad, but I can't take it back and I won't stop now. "Timmy. Where is my daughter?" I'm sitting on his father's desk with my legs spread and he is just standing there staring at me like I am some undefined animal. I know she is dead, in my heart I know it but I need to hear the words and I will hear them one way or another, either from his lips or his parents

4

I stand and tug the skirt of my dress into place before hammering on the wall as I had intended to do in the first place. I can hear him fumbling and the quiet metal of his zipper then the shocked gasp as the panel in the desk pops open. "Don't even think it. Your daddy promised this to me a long time ago. Go ask him. And his left eyelid twitches when he lies."

My purse is more than ample to carry the contents. They have changed over the years; less bejeweled pretty things. to my regret, but much more cash and several bonds. The only thing that didn't make sense was the key in the bottle and I took it anyway. "Junie? I don't know where she is. Victor took her out of here after Dad killed Asher. I'm sorry, for what it's worth. I liked him." I didn't expect an answer at all and my hand freezes over the opening of my bag. Victor was a spoiled, well lawyered and court determined non compos mentis, certifiably nuts. My poor baby.

"Why should I believe you? You stood there and watched him do it. Your mother told me how your father laughed like a child when he told her about it," I said quietly. I meant it to sting, to cut him with my knowledge but my voice can't carry the weight of my disappointment or of my hurt. The tiny clink of the bottle and key seems so final in this tight space and I really don't want to be in here with him anymore.

"I'm going to kill your parents. Both of them once I get some answers. I'm giving you until dark to make arrangements for your children, Tiff and yourself." My purse is heavier than I expect and I stagger a bit when I stand.

"June, for God's Sake, will you listen to me? I didn't have time to say anything let alone move. Asher was telling Dad that he was taking you away, his new job came with a promotion and a move; he told Dad how he planned to surprise you with it when you got home that night when I walked into the office. I was shocked to see him there and Dad pulled that old revolver that he said didn't work from under his desk. He was gone before I could do anything."

Promotion? A move away from here and freedom? More of the thievery that has plagued my life because of Timmy Kartish. "Is this where Asher's brains stuck to the wall Timmy?" I scream, slapping my palm on the new paneling, "Here? Or here?" The tears escape when I'd fought so hard to keep them trapped. Then his arms are around me and he is speaking rapidly in my ear, begging me to listen and understand. "And you let your brother take our daughter, knowing what he was. Let me go Timmy. You have your family to attend to and I have a job to finish." His arms fall from around me and take the little warmth I had felt in forever with them. Olivia is shouting in the lobby and her voice echoes back to where we stand still close but separated by the elephant in the room.

"This is the last chance I'm giving you," I offer, pausing in the doorway with my back to the room, "Where is my daughter? Where did Victor bury her? I have a right to know." There is no response other than the tired sigh of a man tired of talking and I leave him there in the room where Asher died with the knowledge that the deaths of his parents were on his head.

Tiffani had been a blabbermouth who had forced me to react impulsively and I would not make the same mistake again. Olivia looks up at me with suspicious eyes when I re-enter the lobby with my purse now noticeably full and my eyes noticeably dry. Pops' head turns back towards me with cold eyes and his hands clutching his seeping leg with an angry glare. "I've given your son two chances to give me the information I want. He has refused. I'm asking you Daddy-o, one spin all or nothing. Where is my daughter?"

Patriarch Pete's eyes slip to half mast, and glaze over slightly and this will not do. I place the barrel of the gun to Olivia's forehead, pressing hard between her eyes and raise my eyebrows at him in question. "June don't do this. I told you no one knows where your little girl is, but I will help you find her if you just stop this. Please Junie, I know you're angry but they're old and they don't know anything. Just let them be, and I'll help you. I promise." Timmy is standing behind me and his touch is chilly on the nape of my neck and not at all gentle. That motherfucker found the gun in his father's desk drawer.

"Olivia, how about you? It doesn't matter if he blows my head off right now, you will still die. My finger is on the trigger and you have ten seconds to tell me something I can use."

The old woman glances at Pete in disgust and shakes her head before meeting my insistent stare. "The key in the bottle that was in his not so secret stash. Victor took her to the summer house where she would be safe and she is with the nanny I hired to keep her safe." The breath I didn't know I had been holding exploded from my chest in relief and dismay. The firm pressure of cold steel fades away from my neck and mine didn't move an inch.

The old bitch laughs slapping her hand against Pop's chest as though he had told the funniest joke of his life, then sobers enough to spit at me. "Did you really think we would let you keep her June? Asher wasn't her father; we introduced you to him so that it wouldn't look improper while Timmy got his shit together. I'm sure that Victor had some fun with her before he came home again."

Pops still hadn't moved and is watching her through his slitted eyelids, his pallor waxy and lax. The old fuck slipped away while we weren't watching.

Timmy is beside me, his father's gun in his hand pointed at the ground. "Is it true June?" I had no designs to ever tell him that Dexie was his daughter, but his mother had destroyed that plan in short order. I nod and put a little more pressure on the trigger. "They threatened me the second they found out. The day you fucked off and abandoned me for greener pastures or a younger snatch I found out that I was pregnant. That dinner you were supposed to show up for? Surprise! It's a girl."

I take a deeep breath and shout as Timmy's index finger tighten, "wait! You need to know the rest. The last letter I received before Asher had come into this den of iniquity to came on bank letterhead and attached to a thick stack of papers. Dexie was a year old then, and you'd just moved back to town with Tiffani and the kids.

The letter stated that I was to sign them forthwith and prepare for a representative of the family to retrieve Dexie the following Friday or they would be sure that legal action was taken to prove her unfit. That was the end for me. His eyes widen as I slip the crumbled and sweat thinned letter from my bra.

He is watching me crumple the letter in my fist, and stares back down the barrel into his mother's eyes. Timmy's hand is on my neck again, and I flick my eyes away and out into the parking lot. The noise is incredible and I stand open mouthed and stunned with my eyes on Olivia, who sways a moment with her hands at her throat and falls heavily to the floor.

Timmy throws the spent weapon onto the cooling body of his father and walks out the front door and into the midst of those fucking idjits they gave weapons to.

5

Chief Sawton is speaking animatedly with Timmy, waving his pudgy hands around excitedly and grabbing his balding pate with his hands in frustration when Timmy shakes his head resignedly. Looping the strap of my purse across my middle, I snap a new magazine into the gun and push the glassless door frame open, taking aim at the two buffoons closest to me and drop them all before they can draw their own weapons. The world stops making sounds as I pull the trigger again and again, the bodies falling like boneless bloodied sacks to the ground.

The three ogling the slut who had scratched my car look over surprised and the expression doesn't fade as they collapse to the ground to lie in their brains and blood. The crowd is now running amok now, milling in a roiling mass of confusion and fear and the perfect cover for me.

My high heel shoes click on the pavement, adding their odd percussion to the din, and it is all I can hear over the steady beating of my heart. I spy the Chief waddling as quickly as he can between the parked vehicles; Sweat is dripping from under his cap, making him shine in the sun like a suckling pig.

All around me people are calling out for others and in one case, standing stock still and howling with her hands over her ears. The snatch who scratched my car. Her eyes are closed tight, clamped so tight in fact that her eyes are wrinkled at the corners; they pop open when the cold steel of my gun settles on her third eye with childlike wonder. With relish, I cock the hammer and smile sweetly, snarling, "You scratched my car." She shakes her head slowly back and forth with her hand on the keys that still hang from her belt loop, wobbling on those too high heels in fear. I observe with amusement the dark stain spreading from her crotch.

Chief Sawton in my peripheral vision, his hands on his weapon and I hear the click of the hammer. Son of a bitch, he is a sneaky bastard and I give him credit for cleverness.

Feigning capture, I lower the gun and see the girl fall to her knees and watch while the first tears fall into her impressive cleavage. It doesn't go unnoticed by any of the men standing around either.

I want to die; watching the child sobbing on the ground makes me deeply sad for her, and for her parents. An explosion close to me startles me out of my reverie and I brace for the burn of a bullet, tired of this bullshit. When the burn doesn't come, I turn breathless to see Timmy walking toward the two remaining officers with a smile as he pulls the trigger again and again. I was so sure he had run again.

"Junie, be a good girl now and drop the gun. Haven't you done enough?" Sweet Jesus, I had let Chief Sawton get behind me and I feel that tickle itch of a weapon trained between my shoulder blades. It's my own fault for becoming lost in the distraction. Dexie is the only thing on my mind when I feel a clammy hand on my wrist and the cold metal of handcuffs. What an idiot he is, not to disarm me first.

All around us is a ballet of terror, the unifying or perhaps quantifying emotion that brings all these people together is fear, and I caused it. Timmy is watching nearby, the left edge of his lip lifting up and down. "Chief? You are truly a buffoon. It's a wonder you are able to dress yourself in the morning," I laugh, turning on my heel into his surprised face, "Goodbye." There would be no dancing for him as there had been for Victor. In fact, I am sure that several of his colleagues and his wife would vomit on first sight. His surprisingly delicate fingers play a mindless tune on the pavement with his feet keeping time in an oddly fitting end.

Standing over the body of the man I had essentially hobbled, his left knee missing from the knee and still leaking, I survey the melee. Tommy is standing next to me now, urging me to finish this one so we can get out of here and to Dexie and my heart leaps at the thought of my baby girl in my arms again. The slut who scratched my car is still on her knees, still staring at me, her tears staining her cheeks and her eyes flickering between the legless man at my feet and his face as he looks up my skirt with wide eyed interest.

Somethings never change and I am getting tired of hearing his bitching. A squealing sound from the nearby road snaps my attention back to reality and I hand Timmy the purse and the keys. "Go get the car." He grabs my bag and runs, the keys jingling merrily in his fist. Below me, the man that had been enjoying the free show runs his cruor streaked hand up my inner thigh, as I raise my own, pistol in hand and trained on the woman cop that has sped into the parking lot. Several people jump out of the way, staring opened mouthed at the car before running off again.

My last bullet takes the woman cop in the throat, effectively stopping her from sending one of hers into my skull. Her head explodes from her neck and bounces off the still flashing cherries on the top of her car where it splits apart in bits of mealy pink mush and bright scarlet. She stands for a moment, her body, then crumples into a heap under the open door.

I am aroused, damp from the excitement, and from my efforts. I can feel the cop's hand on my thigh, the fingers straining towards what he wishes he could have.

He is muttering low, his mouth opening and closing in soundless words. Dropping to my knees, I settle my ass on his heaving chest and feel his lungs struggle to breathe under my weight, negligible though it is. "Please," he rasps and I stroke his cheek gently, while pulling the small, exquisitely sharp blade from my garter.

Timmy is honking the horn, two beeps then a longer, more impatient blast. Sensuously I touch the boy in blue, taking the time to reach my hand back to feel the size of his package. I wish I could save him for a time, but that is impossible. Dexie. Her name beats in my heart and in my veins. Gently wrapping my fingers in his hair, I force his neck back and slide my blade through the soft meat of his throat. He bucks under me, his hands slipping in the gush of hot read fluid that coats me and it smells richly of salted copper and sulfur.

"Come on June! This is no time to play," Timmy calls from the driver's seat of my 'Cuda with an indulgent smile, and he leans over to open the door for me. Rising to my feet, I point to the girl with a savage smile and she her recoil. Good.

My car smells of Dexie, her sweet clean scent transports me to where I hoped she was playing in the surf and laughing. Timmy squeezes my crimson gloved hand and puts the pedal to the floor.

6

Three days later

The sun is rising over the ocean, turning it from a dark abyss into a firestorm and we are sitting in the driveway of a well-maintained home on the edge of the water, Timmy's arm around my waist and I shiver in the chill ocean morning air.

We travelled without stopping, short of bathroom breaks and to gas up. I cleaned up in the bathroom on our first stop, nearly gagging from the reek of old blood. There wasn't a lot I could do about my hair except rinse it in the filthy sink, and I watched the water flush out red for what felt like hours before it became a faded pink. Still, I felt more human in clean clothes and washed down. Timmy was waiting with the door open and two coffees in the console. My Hero.

I jumped out of the car the second it was safe enough to do so, and ran for the water, pulling my clothes off in desperation. I could her him laughing when I tripped and fell face first into the salty warm heaven. It was a purge, a soul cleansing, and I sobbed while I swam.

I'm not a monster – I never have been. The fact that I murdered, in cold blood admittedly, nine human beings with families and friends who are likely outraged, doesn't make me bad. *Sometimes*, I think, leaning against the man I love, *we are too controlled. Sometimes it's the lack of action that drives us to react* and so I count those casualties as those unavoidable. There are several less evil souls walking the earth this morning, and I am good with that.

"She will be up soon. Are you ready for that?" I murmur against his neck, bracing for a sudden change of heart and relaxing when he kisses my forehead. I can feel his smile. "Any regrets? Your mother… the kids?" Timmy looks me in the eye with dead seriousness and shakes his head gravely.

"Tiff's parent were glad to take them and they were happy to go. They were never really mine and you know that. Olivia? She wasn't my mother. That woman raised me, as you know, with an iron fist covered in diamonds, but she didn't love me. That she saved for Victor. My mother died, at birth, my father said.
I have no information to the contrary." The door behind us flies open and a woman calls out to Timmy with delight, and he turns from me in anticipation. "June. Junie, there she is. Can I-? Do you want to –"" He doesn't wait for my answer and sprints up the stairs towards my raison d'etre and the daughter that he didn't know he had.. I can hear his laughter and can the see tears on his cheek when Dexie reaches out her little hand and grasps his finger, then holds her arms out to him.

A new day and the new start to a life that should have been this way from the start. I mourn for Asher, my heart breaks for the man that was there for me when I was at my lowest and loved me for it. He became a father to Dexie before she was even born; he died needlessly for me and for Dexie. She will know about her other dad, as it should be.

I leave them to bond a moment and wander along the veranda to view the wide area of land we were on. We might be alright here. If there is a God, I hope he will look over us, and forgive me for my failures. It was all in the name of good. I hear Dexie call me Mumma and Timmy's falsetto follow and can't help but smile. Even, As for me, even as I join my little family and step inside the house that would be my home for however long we have together, I worry that one day I will look out one of these windows to a yard full of police cars

Should that day come, I will without regret, take every soul there to protect my family.

ABOUT THE AUTHOR

I am a Canadian based writer who resides in Calgary, Alberta and am a Warrior Mom blessed with two challenging boys, Sam 14 and Davey 10. I am a rabid supporter of Independent Film and Publications, and a horror junkie with a taste for words, and bloodsauce. Most recently, I was voice talent to The Carmen Theatre Group as Maria Sanchez and I can be seen in The Orphan Killer 2: Bound x Blood, written and created by Matt Farnsworth.

Made in the USA
Middletown, DE
02 June 2018